I0623021

# PUCK ME ALWAYS

A JERICHO CHIMERAS ICE HOCKEY DARK
OBSESSION ROMANCE

## SOFIA AVES

LITTLE QUAIL PRESS

First Edition

Published by Little Quail Press

ISBN E: 978-1-922448-73-6

P: 978-1-922448-78-1

## CONTENT WARNING

PUCK ME ALWAYS started as a fast paced, super sexy hockey romance...and devolved from there. This book has a stack of dark themes and content including on page sexual assault, explicit scenes and harsh language. Shannon Incarsen has some questionable morals, including a stalking habit and an unhealthy obsession for his ex-wife. The plot doesn't always travel quite the expected path, so if you're game to risk the wrath of the Incinerator (yes, I had an Arnie-level giggle, too) then turn the page.

Or don't.

At your own risk.

*Sofia xx*

# CHAPTER ONE

## LORI

Fans packed the metrodome, most wearing Jericho Chimeras ice hockey paraphernalia, and the occasional one bearing posters featuring my ex's face.

Life sized.

Like being here wasn't already the most confronting moment of my day. Week.

*Three years.*

It had been that long since Shannon Incarsen walked out on me after I told him I couldn't do the weekly games and have a career in law. That, to his eyes, was the ultimate betrayal. I wouldn't support him–a lie, because I did everything to push his career before he was signed to the Chimeras–but needing extra work time to myself tipped the scales for my ex.

Another lie, because we were exes in name only. Neither of us put the paperwork through to divorce, and technically, we were still married. It suited him because he could focus on hockey alone, without distraction though I never expected it of him. And it suited me because, well...I kept on hoping he'd come back through my door, because no way was I haunting his.

But that never happened.

Tonight, the sheaf of papers in my hands declared me officially the enemy. Any one of his fans would happily lynch my and take my place, offering their own necks to his over-inflated sense of ego and self-worth.

Pulling my shoulders back, I paced with the crowd, avoiding their chants and fangirling efforts as I headed for the locker rooms, only to be stopped by a security guard whose face lit up the moment he spotted me.

"Miss Lori Butler. Now there's a face I never expected to see again." Seamus' lined face beamed at me. "All ready for tonight's game?" He filled out his uniform a little better than before, his hair a little whiter, but his Chimera cap said exactly where his loyalties lay, as always.

Consistency was important to Seamus. He was devastated when I split with Shannon. Or he split with me. An argument could be made either way.

"I mean, sure?" I tucked the papers under my arm. "Is he about?"

"Coach hasn't started talking yet, so he'll be

horsing around." Seamus winked at me. "Gonna play doorman for me while I hunt him down for you?"

I smiled wanly. "I'd appreciate it. Thank you." That sense of impending betrayal and general doom swirled in my gut as I leaned against the door frame and kept my head down, making eye contact with nobody.

Right up until a pair of red heels appeared in my line of sight. "You don't look like one of their usual puck bunnies."

I glanced up into the face of a blindingly blonde woman with lipstick to match her heels. "I'm just waiting."

She flipped her hair and dismissed me in one, her tight white mini skirt and black top that showed more skin that it covered flashing me with an excess of glitter. "Good."

Without a second glance she started down the corridor behind me where Seamus headed.

"I don't think you're allowed down there," I said quietly.

She stopped, though she didn't look back. "What makes you say that? You don't know who I am."

I smiled at her back. "No. But if Coach sees you

in his training area or you interrupt his pep talk, you'll be banned from games for a lifetime."

*And then how will you get on team puck bunny?*

I didn't say that seeing as I was about to get myself booted out of the stadium and Shannon's life forever. I knew how he'd see the request, tell me I could have dated but I couldn't do it. He might have walked out and not come back, but neither of us seemed to really want to end it. At least, I hadn't. Who knew what went on in the 'Incinerator's' head?

Certainly not me, not for a long time.

"He'll be right out." Seamus jogged back toward me, catching the other girl's arm and pushing her away without uttering a single word to her. He puffed a little, bending at the knees. "Sorry, Miss Lori. Just a few minutes, yeah?"

I smiled gently. "Seamus, those puck bunnies are going to run rings around you."

He laughed, a twinkle in his eye. "Who's to say I don't take my own bunnies home, hey?"

"What a rogue." I grinned outright.

The Chimeras' home games were always fun, and the staff were more like family for the years that I watched every game while my work pile grew taller and taller. It was when I nearly fell asleep before a

court date I realised something had to change, and…
here we were.

But the reason for the divorce papers wasn't just work. I needed to socialise, and I wanted to share a bed with someone, even if we worked long hours or the other got up early to train. I just didn't want to be alone anymore.

Selfish, pathetic, and mouse-quiet outside of the courtroom.

Yep, stellar stuff for a Chimeras' WAG, said no pro-hockey player ever.

"Lori." My ex's rich, lowered voice reached me before he did.

Despite not having seen him for three years in person, Shannon's bulky silhouette was the stuff of familiar dreams.

*He's a ten, but he wants me to be something I'm not.*

"I'm sorry," I started, and winced.

He hated when I said *I'm sorry,* like it was a shield against the world. Wanted me to be taller, and stand up for myself. But his arena wasn't my playground, and there was only one place I felt taller.

Spoilers: it was never beside him.

"It's cool." He frowned, raking one hand through his hair, azure eyes surveying me head to toe like he checked I was all there. "Are you okay?"

I stared at him. Whatever I expected him to say, it wasn't that.

*Who are you, and where is the egotistical Shannon Incarsen I fell for?*

But that was a long time ago. And I knew he would hate the part that came next. Or at least, I thought he would.

My stomach clenched up, and I pretended I was back in court, persuading a judge to free a couple from their marital bonds.

It was what I specialised in, after all.

Messy divorces.

I just hadn't expected to have to perform one for myself.

"I have these and I need you to sign them." I held out the sheaf of papers at waist height, trying for both of us to be discrete. "I didn't know where to find you after the house was sold."

He didn't so much as blink. "You look good."

Distracted, I glanced down at my knee length, black denim skirt, and pale pink knitted top that sat loosely over the tops of my thighs with its puffy sleeves. My dark hair hung to the middle of my back, brushed by not done and no skerrick of makeup covered my face.

The only jewelery I wore was my wedding ring

on a chain around my neck, hidden by the sweater in a strategic choice.

The stuff of puck bunnies I looked not.

"I know it's not what you expect." I swallowed, trying to tear my gaze from his, but how does one *not* drool over the most droolworthy hockey player on earth?

*Why did I leave, again?*

That's right, because I didn't have an identity next to Shannon. Because all I wanted to do was support him to the detriment of my own life. Yes, it was a me problem. And that was why I stood in front of him right where I shouldn't be, less than fifteen minutes before a game.

*I should have gotten someone else to do this.*

"From you I do expect so much," he mused, taking a step forward into my space. "That's true. How's your career going, Lori?"

Every time he said my name I swore something took a deep dive in my stomach.

"It's great." I frowned, trying to get back on track. "I–"

"Come out to dinner with me," he said in a low voice, ignoring Seamus fidgeting off to one side. "I miss you."

Tears tried to spring to my eyes, but I didn't have

the energy to give them prime real estate. "I know you don't have time. I need you to take these, sign them and send them to my lawyer. They're div–"

"With me." He grabbed my elbow, sending me a hard glance that told me to hold it in until we were alone.

Shannon nodded to Seamus as he dragged me right past the befuddled security guard who might or might not have been trying to eavesdrop on our little domestic scene and right into the first door he tried that opened, pushing me inside.

I stood in the middle of a janitor's cupboard, staring at various cleaning paraphernalia, and placed my hands on my hips, pivoting to face him. "Maybe dinner would have been better."

"Bullshit. You never went for any of that fancy shit. That's one of the things I always loved about you." He flicked on a light that glowed dimly with the last of its strength.

I envied its tenacity while I gathered my thoughts. Being around Shannon was no different for me than it was for the rest of the world. He was overwhelming, supersized in every way. In personality, in person. He towered over me by a foot and a half, and in photos we'd always been a point of laughter, where he either crouched down with me or picked me up. But in the bedroom, that size different paid itself off when he slid his massive body over my smaller one and–

"Talk to me, Butler," he murmured, using my maiden name as he braced his forearms on either side of the shelves above my head and leaned down to face level with me.

Extra bicep muscles popped out everywhere, and I failed to ignore them.

"Divorce papers," I said firmly, willing my ovaries not to go into overdrive. "I need you to read them and sign. Send them back to your lawyer. Or to me. I'll get the rest done."

Shannon was silent for a long moment as he stared at me, his eyes glittering. "Three years, huh? That's a long time since we've been together."

It was a long time. Three years of torture and hell as my heart broke on my first and only love over and over.

"That wasn't my problem," I said tartly. "I wasn't the one who walked out."

"But my door's been open to you ever since."

My insides froze. "Mine, too," I whispered. "But neither of us ever took that step."

"No. We didn't." Shannon moved forward,

crowding my space in the small, cluttered room that smelled like sanitizer and soggy mops.

"I just came to give them to you," I said through a thick throat. *Not freaking now.* I couldn't lose it. I wouldn't. "I know you've got your game. It's going to start soon."

Shannon growled. He actually freaking growled. "Fuck the game. I haven't seen you in too long."

My heart shattered on the spot. "You're not going to sign them, then?" Why did I have a tick of hope in that? *Why?*

"I'll sign if that's what you want." His face shuttered. "If it's what you really want." He stepped forward, dropping his hands to my hips, his stare fathomless.

I shook my head vehemently, my hair whiplashing my cheeks. "No. You don't get to do this. Not again."

The day he walked out we fought. Hard. Loud. Then we fucked the same way.

And he left anyway.

We put the house up for sale, the one we bought together with income from our first shitty jobs out of college where we met before he was drafted. We sold the memory of our struggle to make it, and both of us walked away.

Not a single remnant of our past together remained, except when we were together.

My skin tingled at his proximity. I shook my head hard when he didn't stop, working his fingers under my knit top and grazing his fingertips against my sides. His thumbs made a little rhythm I recognised. I hated that my breath hitched, wanting him. *Craving* him like some addiction I couldn't quit.

This was that day.

"I have a date," I said firmly, shoving the papers into his midsection.

Shannon didn't so much as *oof*.

"A date." His voice flattened. "Now, when I have a game?"

I blinked at him. "Um, no. About an hour after it'll finish, I think? I have to go home and get ready." I clamped my mouth shut before I could spill the tea on anything else about my life I didn't want him to know.

"Good." His voice was all cat's got the cream as he backed me up until the shelving dug into my back. "We have time, then."

"For what?" I frowned at him. "You can't read the papers here. The light's shit. And it will take ages."

"Not that." His lips curled into the ghost of a sinful smile. "I trust you not to screw me over, Lori.

It's why I never pushed you." His hands landed on the shelf behind my head. "But I didn't know you were dating."

"I– it's new," I lied.

It was my first date since college, since him, though technically as we hooked up at a frat party, I'd never been on a date. Shannon assimilated me into his life and that was it. I just became another fixture, until the day I wasn't.

"New," he mused, dipping his head until his breath brushed my lips. "How new, Lori?" Those same lips touched the corner of my mouth and held there in an intimate gesture that left my skin trembling with gooseflesh.

"Stop it." I shoved my hands filled with the divorce papers at his chest, unsure how long my resolve would last.

"What's he like?"

*As far from you as I could get.*

"He's an accountant. Steady job. Not after promotions. Zero ego."

"Probably not the strongest man to look after you, then." His teeth bared.

"I don't need that," I countered. "Besides, he seems to love you almost as much as you love yourself."

That part didn't sit so well with me, the way Dave went on and freaking *on* about Shannon, but then, half of the US was obsessed with him. Why should I expect any less of a date?

"Is that what you think of me?" His voice dripped with sin.

"Not like this again, Shannon."

He drew back, catching my wrists and rubbing his thumbs over my pulse point that I knew would give me away if he paid attention. "You remember."

It would be hard to forget the best and only sex of my life, so I said nothing.

"You do." His body pressed against mine, engulfing me with the overbearing hugeness of everything about him. "That good, huh?" The smugness I recognised on his face shit me instantly.

"You'd think so. Not that you'd know, because wasn't that the day you walked out?"

The ego dropped from his face to be replaced by a frown. "That was a mistake. I missed you."

I glared at him. "Past. Tense, Shannon. Can you say you actually miss me?" Doubt thrived in my head.

"No," he shook my head, and disappointment roiled around my mind so that I almost–*almost*– missed what he said afterward. "But I'll show you."

# CHAPTER TWO

## SHANNON

Lori Incarsen-nee-Butler was the kryptonite ripping through my veins.

She'd always been there, since college, when I was the hot shot prodigy with the hopes of everyone around me desperately waiting for the moment *it* happened. An early draft. She was there, all the way through those days when I barely slept, trained my ass off, and got my first pro game in.

She was there when I played for several bottom rungers, and she was there when I pulled my first seven-figure contract with the Chimeras.

After that was when I lost her. Our careers clashed, and we barely had time to eat, sleep and piss, let alone love each other properly. And yet for the last three years my bed had been empty without her in it.

I've watched her, though she doesn't seem to know it. Hasn't returned the favor.

And now she wants to go out on a fucking date with some brown-suit fanboy.

*Good fucking luck with that.*

Her face went blank, and my lips became wet. I might have snarled at her a little. Wouldn't change what I was about to do, though. The moment she pulled that little stunt–the date, not the divorce papers–I knew I'd do anything to push her limits. Remind her who we were together, who we *are*.

Three years, and nothing's changed. She's still the college girl from next door, the one who got me hard the moment she smiled at me with those liquid brown eyes and hair the perfect length to wrap around my fist while I fucked her and reminded her who she belonged to.

*Tonight won't be any different.*

She made a mistake seeing me before the game. After, even with a win, I'd be hyped but exhausted. That would last at least until tomorrow.

Right now I had energy to burn.

I swiped the sheaf of papers from her hands, scattering them across the room. Her gasp of outrage or maybe indignation might sting a little on the inside but fuck it–someone else could clean it up later.

My hands landed on her hips before she could slam her palms to my chest, and by the time she did, her skirt inched to her waist, and her ass was planted on the shelf behind. I pressed one hand beneath her, playing with her pussy through her panties. It wasn't her palms but her fists that smashed into my chest, but she could have punched me in the face for all it would do to prevent what happened next.

Her shocked cries turned to moans as she drenched her panties. I cupped her jaw, holding her head tilted back as I played with her through the sopping material.

"Wet already, Lori? What sort of date is this you're going on?"

Her head came up–tried to, but I didn't let her move an inch.

"Don't stop," she moaned, her lips parting and her sweet breath grazing my lips.

"Don't stop?" My smile turned wicked. "I thought a moment ago you said no."

Confusion crossed her gaze, and she was oh so fucking beautiful in that moment, falling apart in my hands.

"I–" Her brow dipped and those hands hammering my chest gripped my shirt, fisting it into knots as she pulled me forward. "I need you, Shannon. Now." The tiny demand slipped past her lips, but she was so far gone she didn't seem to notice.

*"My pleasure."*

I gripped her panties and ripped hard, shredding

the material only to go back to playing with her. Fuck if I didn't want her pussy spasming around me from one orgasm only to give her another the moment I entered her. I knew this woman, called her mine for too many years not to know the depths of her pleasure and all of her secrets.

"Christ," she whispered as I pushed two fingers into her sopping cunt, inching forward to impale herself, rocking with me.

"Close, baby?" I gripped her jaw tighter, wanting to mark her.

Needing to know her date would ask about the bruises and that her face would flush prettily as she denied everything in a soft voice while her thighs gushed traitorously at the memory of what we did now.

I found her clit and spread her wetness all over, slicking the tiny nub already hard and tight. *Too easy. Too stunning.*

"Shannon–" Her gaze grew wild as she met mine.

I let out a growl that ripped at my throat. "Why are you looking at your ex-husband like that, Lori? Gonna get yourself in trouble."

She shivered in my arms and came for me, breaking and shattering and so fucking stunning. I bent down to kiss her, letting go of her jaw the moment my mouth connected with hers, but a simple kiss was never my plan. I shoved my tongue into her mouth, loving the way her body arched for me, her pussy fluttering madly around my fingers as the aftershocks of bliss rocked her.

I pulled my cock out, removing my fingers and replacing them with what she needed so badly in seconds. Her moans grew louder. Once, I might have cared who heard, but right now I needed to hear her come again.

Preferably while riding my cock.

"Ready, baby?" I purred, sucking and licking my way along her neck.

She had a sweet spot in the crook of her neck she always tried to hide from me. I dived in, marking her skin until she rocked with me as I fucked her hard enough that the cleaning equipment on the shelf behind her started to topple.

"I can't– you know that–" she stuttered, her entire body shaking.

I put my hands to good use, one gripping the curve of her ass tight, the other cupping the back of her neck, rubbing circles there. Overloading her body and mind was my favourite game. Seeing her fall for me came second.

"You can. Actually, you're going to go to your date

tonight, your panties ruined, with my cum trailing down your thighs." My voice came out ragged as I screwed us both into oblivion. "And maybe if you take him home and fuck him, I'll make sure the next time I see you it'll be your ass I drown in my cum. Wanna go on a date with another man while your husband's cum trickles down your thighs, Lori?" I cooed, railing her with all the excess energy flooding my system.

"You– I can't–" Her eyes went from wild to glazed in a heartbeat, and she milked my cock with her pretty cunt with everything she had.

"Perfect," I groaned as I came inside her raw, glazing her walls and marking her from the inside out.

My shout echoed back at me, then she was in my arms as I held her to my chest, memorizing the feel of the woman I wanted every damn night but didn't let myself have.

Because she said she needed something I couldn't give her, and it hurt like fuck.

This didn't, though. Not even as I tucked her ruined panties into a knot between her legs already dripping with my cum. Not as I straightened her shirt and hair as she clung to me, still shaking and whimpering.

Not as I kissed her hard enough to bruise those perfect lips, leaving her dazed, her *just fucked* face obvious, and pushed her toward the door.

"I'll look at the papers, promise." I kissed beneath her ear and licked there, if only for one last taste of her to savor tonight. "I have a game to win. Have fun on your date."

I pushed her out the door and had the singular joy of watching her stumble toward the exit while poor old Seamus tried not to watch, his face aglow with everything he just heard through the very much not soundproofed door.

Bless, she put her hand on the stadium's glass door, pausing there for a moment, but didn't look back, not even while I waited. Then she disappeared into the night, and I pulled my shit back together and headed to the locker room for my helmet and stick.

It was a turn around on the usual pre-game no sex strategy but fuck me if my blood wasn't fired up enough to trounce a whole fucking team on my own.

In the end it was Coach who tried to trounce me, but I weathered his rage, determined to prove my worth on the ice and did just that, taking out their entire defence before shuttling the biscuit neatly into the basket five times in quick succession.

That earned me less of a scowl from Coach, and plenty of cheer from the team.

The next face off started with trash talk, my favorite kind.

"Heard you got happy in the locker room with a bunny before the game," the captain of the other team sneered. "Thought you were saving your swimmers for me? Wanna kissey-kiss?" He made smooching noises through his helmet.

"Keep talking and you can bend over after I score okay, sweetie? I'll loosen you up real good." I winked at him while he spluttered, and took the puck up the other end.

The night was on fire, or maybe it was simply Lori in my veins that did it. By the end of the game even Coach had a rare smile on his face.

"Keep that up, kid, and we'll be lined up for the playoffs, no problem." His comment wasn't lost on me. I nodded.

"Try to keep it up, sir."

"Good to hear after this evening's false start. Now go home with a bunny for once and make yourself happy."

"Sure I can find something pretty." I turned my back and grimaced at the lie.

Anyone else might have been on the rampage after how Lori and I broke up, but it wasn't in me to screw around. I did that before I met her, but once we were together I never wanted anyone else. They just didn't meet the mark and man, was that mark high. Rather like the ones I left on her neck earlier.

I hoped the date asked about those, too.

Coach alone knew about my self-imposed abstinence, but what he didn't know about was my weekly nighttime routine before I headed home and caught some zzzs.

"Alright. Gotta go." I slapped a few shoulders, promised I'd be at training Monday morning bright and fucking merry, and headed out.

I had a date to crash, though if I had it my way, Lori wouldn't know I was there until I wanted her to know.

If I wanted her to know.

Finding her wasn't a problem. Parking might have been, but I wasn't above using my face to get what I wanted. The sheaf of divorce papers sat on my passenger seat of my McLaren 750S. Call it my pre-midlife crisis or post break up buy, but everything else that came from the sale of the cottage and my wage went into a bank account for a rainy day.

The day I needed to crawl to Lori and beg her to come back to me.

But for now, I was having too much fun torturing the woman I loved to bend the knee just yet. If she was on her back or wanted to ride my face, maybe, but that would be a push. Lori might be confident in what she knew best–law–but that didn't make her confident in general.

It broke me to know I had a hand in that out of pure distraction and ignorance. Because I hadn't watched her enough.

But I spent the past three years watching her on a weekly basis. She might not have seen me in all that time, but I sure as fuck got my weekly fill of her. Enough to stay sane, and keep going.

Which was why tonight's date was interesting. Plus, she lied to me.

Some friends set her up on blind dates that were doomed to fail from the start. She didn't want a distraction or a one-night stand. Nothing horrify her more. Not strange hands on her body or knowing if she was safe. The only risk she liked was my sort, because my risks were calculated to the nth degree. My Lori liked security, and she liked coming home to someone who loved her.

That right there was my failure. Those first years of draft were hard but coming on board with the Jericho Chimeras? That was a whole 'nother level of crazy town. And because of my distraction, I lost her.

Those divorce papers were my countdown timer. I had two weeks to make it work, and get her to burn them–preferably in front of me. Less, if I could manage it.

Tonight would be the start of a brand new campaign.

I tossed my keys to the valet who fumbled them while I pretended not to notice or hear his dozen apologies that flowed out in quick succession. How much of an asshole did I seem that he thought I'd rip him a new one because he nearly dropped my keys, for fuck's sake? Some clientele this place must have.

I frowned as I wanted into the Glace's hotel lobby, noting the chandeliers. Something didn't add up. Didn't Lori say the dude was an accountant? Unless he was working for the mob, then he couldn't afford a place like this, nor get a reservation on short notice.

Like a year's worth of notice.

Christ, how many dating apps was she on? I needed to make a profile and stalk my wife's curvaceous ass down virtually as well as in person. I wasn't sure what I'd find after that, but I saw her and my brain emptied of everything.

Lori changed into a knee length black dress laced with rose gold highlights in tasteful glitter. A dress I fucking bought her for our anniversary, to take her to a place just like this. I had a reservation booked a year in advance because I wasn't famous at the time, and I looked forward to that meal with her I couldn't actually afford back then.

I saw her in that dress, and we ended up in bed and ordered in, taking breaks between fucking and lovemaking for the entire night only to wake in rumpled sheets and do it all over again in the morning sun.

That was before she realized how toxic I was for her career, and I understood how little I knew about her needs, what I missed and ignored, kicking myself for weeks after. Torn between chasing her down and giving her freedom, I threw myself into my hockey career. That got me through the first six months without her.

After that I reverted to a monthly, then weekly

stalking habit, just to check she was okay. She moved a handful of times, and I'd scrape the place clean afterward, collecting the few items she missed and putting them into her garage or moving boxes when no one else was looking.

As far as I knew she had no idea how close I'd been that entire time. Hearing her say she missed me, the longing in her voice tonight, it almost broke me.

But not quite.

I'd find a way to break her, though, and make her beg for everything I needed right back from her. But first, I wanted to see what sort of accountant date could get her into a place like this.

I wandered close enough behind her that she would see me if she turned around, but she never did.

"Mrs Shannon Incarsen, please," she said softly, clutching her purple purse tightly in her hands and flicking the edge with her short, neat nails that were digging into my shoulders a few hours ago.

It was the nails that interested me. Because she only flicked things like that when she was nervous. *How long have you been using my name to your advantage, little wifey?* But when I stared closer, the man on her arm practically jiggled, running his finger down the list and pointing it out to the host who frowned, but didn't say anything.

The man in question wore a brown suit–I expected nothing less–that looked like it was either a hand-me-down, or made of polyester. Surely her date could have made an effort. His hair was pushed back from his face like a fifty's greaser, and the tell-tale square of a cigarette pack sat in his coat pocket.

I grimaced at the break in propriety, knowing she'd hate that habit if he hadn't already told her about it. Smoke made her cough to the point of puking, always had.

My gaze flicked back to the attendant who led them to a table after hosting a hushed conversation with the Matre'd. *Interesting.* So, she wasn't used to using my name, but let this flea of a man speak for her?

Lori might be many things, but she was never a puppet, letting other people's voice come out of her mouth. She always had an opinion, even if she didn't speak it, and would spend hours with me nutting out an argument until it died a long, mangled death.

Those were the nights I enjoyed most, talking shit with her and teasing her until we fell asleep together. Then I carried her to bed in the smallest hours of the morning when I woke in a cramped curl beneath her.

Lori twitched when the waiter pressed a hand to her lower back, and a matching growl rose in my throat, startling the hostess. I wondered if my little wife did as I bid and kept the filthy, ruined panties on, or went home and showered the scent of our frantic fucking off?

A smile spread across my face as I turned away before the hotel staff or my wife could spot me, and disappeared into a shadowy hallway to wait.

## CHAPTER THREE

### LORI

I sat opposite my date having used my ex-husband's name to secure a booking with my thighs glazed with the evidence of our insanity and wondered what in the hell I was doing with my life.

The obvious deviation of the plan was enough to make me question everything, but that little voice inside my head whispered, *why not go back?* But then my career would never matter, and I would fade, along with all sense of self. It was the reason he walked away in the first place.

The second was to quietly extract my hand from Dave's clammy grip, excuse myself before my pale looking date started talking, and make my way to the bathrooms. I closed the door and leaned my head on the cool tile, uncaring if it was hygienic or not.

"What the hell am I doing?" I muttered to myself.

"Getting yourself into trouble, as promised." Shannon closed the toilet door behind him and flicked the lock–which I had failed to do.

He'd changed into a loose black silk shirt that hung from his hard, oversized frame like a king's mantle. Black slacks and shoes completed the look. He ran his thumb across his belt, a knowing look in his eyes I tried not to remember from many years for the rush of heat between my already slicked thighs.

And he fucking well *knew* the effect he had on me when he did that. But a marriage wasn't just about sex. Couldn't be. Had to be more.

The mantra of lies I sold myself by the second.

"You can't be here." I glared at him, shaking my head and backing up. "Too much, Shannon. Personal space."

"While my wife goes on a date with another man? I don't think so." That smile was back, the one that promised dark, dirty things as he crowded my space like he had in the janitor's room at the stadium earlier. "Besides, I might like a meal here tonight, but it looks like my table's already been taken."

I winced. "It was a shitty move and I'm sorry. He pushed, and I didn't think."

His smile sharpened as he blocked the light, his shadow engulfing me. "You're right. You didn't think. Bend over the bench, Lori."

I stared at the plain white marble bench with its potted orchid and shook my head. "No fucking way, Shannon. This is getting ridiculous. I did what you said–" I clamped my mouth and eyes shut, and that was my third mistake of the night.

"Did you? Let me check." His silky voice came from directly in front of me, the asshole having taken the opportunity to close the distance between us when I wasn't looking.

Or maybe it was an invitation I extended in the hope I could claim it was all him.

His hand slid into the slit of my dress, working upward while I stood there with my eyes squeezed shut and saying nothing. Doing nothing.

While he discovered it wasn't just his cum that wet my thighs.

"Very good girl," he said approvingly. "Maybe we don't need the punishment after all."

"Please," I whispered, breathy and pathetic like a fangirl on her first time with a national treasure.

Instead, it was the man I lived with for years who knew how to play my body like an instrument made just for him. That he still wanted me warmed my skin to overheating as I tried not to twist on my four-inch heels that accidentally made me taller than my date.

My breath shortened as I realized he was about to do it again...and that I wasn't going to stop him.

*I'm panting over him. Fuck me.*

"Actually, I might," Shannon purred, brushing his mouth lightly over mine as he played gently between my legs where I ached from the way he rough-fucked me earlier. The need built within me until my knees wobbled. "I gotcha." His hand slid around my waist as he kissed me, holding me up, but his touch was different this time.

Tender, loving.

My mind swirled with a different sort of need, the one that nearly broke my heart as he stroked the tip of his tongue across my bottom lip, asking permission.

Permission I granted.

He dipped inside, exploring, reacquainting. This wasn't anything like his dominating kisses of before, hours ago when he ripped me apart and put me back together in a mould he liked best. This was a soft request as he lifted me onto the bench, pushing my skirt up and settled between my thighs.

"No need for punishments, right? Because you've always been my good girl." He reached between us, opening my folds and playing there but not bringing me to orgasm before he freed his cock and fed himself inside me inch by excruciatingly torturous inch. "My perfect girl, Lori. Only you."

I let out a moan that could have been a sob and

buried my head in his shoulder, clinging to him. "I shouldn't be doing this. Not again," I whispered, gasping at the end as he surged forward, bottoming out then slowly withdrew to fill me again.

Pain and pleasure spread through me as I clutched to him, already drowning in the way he took over everything about me. Like I'd lose myself if I let go and would never be found again.

His hands flexed on my body but he kept his touch gentle, yet firm, holding me securely so the only pain I felt was from where he stretched me earlier. Sure, I had toys I played with, but I hadn't had sex with anyone else. Hadn't dated, because it felt wrong, like I was reducing any chance of hope.

And now here he was making love to me.

In a hotel bathroom, while another man checked his watch and ordered without me.

A true sob tore through. Shannon cupped the back of my head, holding my cheek to his shirt, mussing the material, my hair, and my make up. Neither of us would leave unscathed, inside or out, but I knew the humiliation of walking through the hotel afterwards would be too much.

"This is what you do to me," I despaired, digging my nails into his shoulders that filled my hands, the slinky material wet with my kisses and my tears.

"I know, baby," he soothed. "I know. Just let me take you apart and it will be alright."

"That doesn't help," I started but he kissed me again like before, and everything–the bathroom, the hotel, the world–it all disappeared as I fell into him.

Shannon felt the moment I surrendered because his hands tightened, his smile sharpened and his thrusts became possessive, driving deeper into me. He leaned me back, arching his body over mine until I almost disappeared, and tilted my hips up to fill me more.

My poor pussy took the abuse like a champ, the damp ends of his silk shirt trailing across my clit with every deep thrust that left my sight blanking bright white.

"No, I don't want to come," I whispered desperately, lying to myself that if I didn't come then I wasn't enjoying what he did to me.

*All the filthy lies.*

"Of course you do, beautiful. You want to soak my cock and mark me like I'm gonna mark you. Only we know, and that's our secret." He kissed the corner of my mouth, digging his thumbs into the corners of my hips where he knew I was so sensitive.

Pleasure speared through me as he bore down, the expression on his face pure rapture as I broke, slathering his cock and my skirt with my juices as I squirted for him.

"Damn I've missed that," Shannon rasped, spearing his fingers through my hair and pulling my head back. "Feeling the flood of wetness that tells me I've loved you right."

"No," I gasped, my cheeks burning, another falsehood on my tongue. "No, Shannon, that's not what it means–"

He kissed me long and hard, cutting off my words and thoughts, his thrusts speeding up. "It means you're mine again. Ever wonder why you never lost anything those times you moved? Your mother's locket you couldn't find? It was caught on the inside of a closet door. And other things I brought back. I never left you, Lori. I couldn't stand to be without you."

"What?" I struggled to put words together. "The movers brought that back."

"Because I gave it to them. I scoured each place, didn't want you to lose anything when you were upset to move again because of work. Further away." He kissed the corner of my mouth, slipping his tongue in to dance with mine as pressure built, gliding out of control at his words. "Sometimes I'd call your cell when you were asleep when it was turned off just to hear your sweet voice on voice mail."

"Shannon, no–"

I choked as his hand wound around the back of my neck, holding me in place as he stared straight into my eyes, unforgiving, unyielding.

"Yes, Lori. I've always been there. Watching you, protecting you. I've been there for you for years even though you've never known. Hell, I've climbed through that bedroom window of yours in that tiny cottage you bought to try to replace ours and stood there watching you sleep more times than I can count."

"What?" My orgasm hurtled toward me, nothing he said making sense. "Shan–"

"I touched you, Lori. Couldn't keep my hands to yourself. Ever wake up wet between your thighs like you had a dirty dream you couldn't remember?"

"I–" I had woken like that, for weeks in a row. My body soaked in sweat, my clit still throbbing, unsated. I got up those mornings and showered, then used my favorite vibe to ease the pressure before I made it to work.

"Never alone. Not once," he murmured.

My breaths increased as comprehension hit me. He stalked me–was in my house while I slept. The illusion of freedom was just that, a mirage I created in a desperate bid at independence I never really achieved.

Because he was there.

A scream built in my throat as my orgasm slammed into me with all the grace of a runaway train. Shannon's mouth was there on mine, swallowing the sounds he tore from me as he came inside me again.

I shuddered in the circle of his arms, resting my face to his chest where he held me, his hips rocking still, pushing his cum deeper.

"So beautiful. My girl," he said tenderly in all the wrong but good, best of fucked up ways as he withdrew, tucking himself way and curled a strand of hair behind my ear. "I'll see you soon, okay?"

His promise was the last thing I heard, his tender kiss the last touch, before the bathroom door opened and closed before him, leaving me alone with his cum dripping along my thighs for the second time in the same day.

My date didn't last long. I could barely sit at the table with my knees pressed together, let alone follow the flow of the one-sided conversation Dave kept up with his accounting anecdotes and meaningless facts and figures.

"Aren't you going to eat, Loreli?" Dave used the name I hated since birth and requested he didn't use, but my senseless date forgot and used it anyway.

*Loreli Incasren.* A name that opened doors no matter how long we'd been apart or hadn't been photographed in public.

Hell, if a picture was taken of me with this loser, Shannon's name would be all over the news without mercy. And it would be my doing why he didn't concentrate on his game and fought the paps instead.

But also...why did I care?

I ignored the accountant and gestured to a waiter, ordering a magnum of champagne. If Shannon wanted to watch, he could because for the first time in so long I wanted to break all the rules, and no longer be boxed in by anyone.

Being fucked by your ex in a public–if decently clean–toilet did that.

The champagne arrived and I finished my glass only for it to be refilled the moment I finished. The waiter's kind, brown eyes held a fraction of sympathy. I wondered if he saw tortured couples constantly in this high end lifestyle, each tethered to one another and unable to escape.

I thought I had escaped, and look where that got me.

"Ahem," Dave twiddled his glass stem and looked pointedly at the waiter.

I covered a giggle that bubbled up behind pursed lips that probably made my face look like a cat's ass for all I knew, with my messy hair and just-fucked face. The waiter glanced at me for permission.

My nod and two fingers gave him all the access he needed before he poured and set the magnum of champagne in an ice bucket.

"Don't you think he should have poured for me, too? I'll have a word with the manager." Dave puffed his chest out like the self-important man he thought he was.

I sighed, said a silent prayer for the waiter's continued employment, and let bubbles and good food drown out my date's endless chatter that went on and on about nothing at all. I couldn't wait to escape to my home, a large part of me aching for Shannon's return. It was like now that I'd had more of him, I couldn't get enough.

But the way he pushed himself into my existence told me what life would be like with him again...and neither of us would survive a second round of that, either in career or in our hearts.

I knew that, even if he wouldn't admit it to himself.

And so when I went home, alone, I locked all the windows and doors that night, and each after, learning to sleep in an airless room, confined in a cell of my own making, hopeful of the man who would knock on my door.

But I never saw him that night, or any after for the next week. And that broken promise had me shuffling those newly printed divorce papers so often the pages curled at the corners, and my signature on the bottom grew steadily more aggressive.

# CHAPTER FOUR

## SHANNON

Watching Lori slowly lose her mind when I wasn't where she expected for the past week had been my favourite new game to play, driving me to utter distraction. Thankfully there was no real game scheduled for this weekend, which meant I could take my time and torture her slowly before I reeled her back in.

Because that was the goal. I didn't want to be without her any longer.

Seeing her struggle through her date, getting progressively drunker, was a bad idea on her part. Because she knew I was watching her, and so she let down her guard, but what if I went home and held a pity party on my own? What would she do then when her accountant's hands wandered, and I didn't turn up on call? No, that's not the rules we played by.

I chose when my obsessive need to feel her skin beneath my hands raged, and she let me in, just like she had the last two times she submitted to me. It was the perfect balance, if only I could show her it would work around her needs this time.

Fuck, I was desperate to prove she'd have time for her career and get enough sleep. Mine was established, and that crazy period of my life was over. She just needed to see that, and I wanted to show her.

In my bed or hers, I didn't care.

Our relationship had always been based around a deep, burning need for each other. It hadn't been half as frantic back then, and we took time discovering each other, trying out a few kinks along the way. Most we discarded as they just didn't fit who we were. But a couple stayed. She loved my hand around her throat when I was balls deep in her, and she moaned and gushed when I spanked her.

But mostly she came hard when I surprised her and didn't give her a chance to say no. That's what I banked on tonight.

Afterwards I'd spoil her like the queen she was for me, making sure she knew how much I adored her. When I walked away in the stupidest decision of my life, I screwed up what we had. The perfect nights, the mornings drenched in sunlight making love and feeding her until she protested.

Just holding her and studying every aspect of her face so my body would know hers blindfolded.

That's the sort of love I was certain we still shared and if not...If I was wrong, then she was about to get the sort of surprise that gave her a different sort of happiness, even if it might be unwelcome at first.

I slipped between the stunted roses she didn't have the time to care for and shouldered open the cracked window in her spare room. I wasn't sure if she forgot this one or left it ajar for me on purpose. That could go either way, but I was grateful I didn't have to use the key I copied from her handbag the last time she moved.

That made her use her spare key for a week, and rather than take that, I made my own copy for a rainy day. I hadn't needed it yet, but that didn't mean it wouldn't come in handy at some point.

Pushing my way through the window, I slipped into the spare room, my shoes making little sound on her thick carpet that felt like it hadn't ever been used in this room. Lori didn't have much contact with her family after law school, and our marriage and then break up cemented her dislike of the lack of support that came her way.

I didn't blame her on that front, but I was pleased not to find bad-date-Dave snoozing in her house.

My blood boiled at the thought of her with another man as I padded across the hall and straight into her room. The door wasn't closed, though her bedroom window was shut. I smiled at the memory of the last time I was in this room, curling up beside her to sleep.

"Not tonight, baby," I murmured, falling to my knees beside her bed.

Lori curled beneath a twisted sheet, like she couldn't get comfortable, her legs tucked around the edges. She'd always hated a closed window, so I rose again and shoved it open a few inches, just to let in fresh air.

The change in her was instantaneous. Her feet stretched out, and the lines on her pretty face softened. I crouched next to her, trailing my fingers along her side, taking some of the thin cotton nightie she preferred along with my touch until the tops of her legs were bare. I stared at the trimmed patch of dark hair between her legs and smirked. The last time I was here she was au natural–nary a trim in sight.

"That little bit of gardening had better be for me, baby," I murmured, tracing featherlight patterns across the tops of her thighs.

Lori sighed in her sleep, settling with her legs spread a little, a beautiful invitation from a beautiful woman. I kissed her skin where I touched her then moved up her body to find her mouth, covering her lips gently with mine.

Her breath stalled for a moment. I coaxed her lips apart, kissing her deeply as she started to stir. One of her hands came up to catch my hair, running her fingers across the back of my neck, and I let one of my hands slide between her legs in return, fingering her damp pussy lips, teasing her open.

Her legs parted as she moaned when I found her clit, turning slicked circles there. She leaned into my kiss, opening her mouth wider when I thrust my tongue deeper, to the point of discomfort. Her mumbled protest as she roused spurred me on. I found her entrance and pushed two fingers deep inside her, groaning aloud at the warmth of her.

It was like that sound from me slammed her into reality. Her pussy clenched on my fingers, and she bore down, her hips working rhythmically, knowing what she wanted well before her dozy mind caught up in the small hours of the night when dirty things happen.

"Shannon," she whispered. "You- you weren't here."

"I'm here now, baby." I drew back just long enough to see her eyes, then I kissed her again, pumping my fingers in and out of her clenching pussy.

A moan left her lips unbidden, her nails digging into my biceps. "Oh, God. You can't–"

"I am," I said firmly. "Come for me, then I'll lick you clean so you can come on my tongue. Promise," I encouraged her, working my fingers faster, but I didn't need to put much effort in.

Her body did the work for me, rocking and pushing down hard onto my hand. I stilled, letting her drag the pleasure out of that first touch of the night. Her orgasm hit slow, but hard.

Her lips parted on breathless air, her lashes fluttering as she came. Those perfect thighs with their curves and edible flesh closed around my forearm as she took what she needed from me, and it was so goddamn beautiful.

"More," she moaned, her eyelashes still fluttering and I swore her eyes rolled.

"All night long, baby." *Maybe tomorrow, too, if you let me stay.*

That was a hell of a jump, and we'd see how well she managed this part first.

"Yes, please," she gasped, her pussy pulsing around my fingers, coating them in her cream, her legs still locked around my forearm.

"Good girl," I praised her, sweeping hair back from her face and cupping her jaw tenderly. "God, I've missed you, Lori. Really fucking missed you."

"Missed you, too." She turned her head to one side and yawned, even as her body trembled for me. "Are you gonna get into bed and keep me awake or let me sleep?"

"Sassy bitch," I said gently, with no heat, and she smiled at me. Harsh words never hurt us; we always knew who we were to each other. But tonight felt like breaking new ground. And that...that scared the absolute shit out of me. "I promised you something."

Kissing her again—God, I'd never get enough of that sweet mouth–I knelt between her legs and licked my way leisurely along her thighs, taking my time to clean the mess she made as she threw her legs over my shoulders, gripping the mattress for balance, like she'd fall off if she didn't hang on.

Around her, I knew that feeling all too well.

"Are you gonna come here and do this every night?" She gasped as I licked around her folds and buried my tongue in her pussy.

Her desperate moan a moment later when I found her clit and suckled the tight bud into my mouth, twirling my tongue around the sensitive nerve bundle, had me straining to be inside her. I had my fill of her before, and tonight needed to be something special. Like we were reestablishing trust.

While I broke into her house and licked her clean.

Sure, there were some inconsistencies there, but I warned her out, and she knew I was coming, if she didn't know *when*. She could have set bear traps, for Christ's sake, but she didn't.

And I swore she left that window open on purpose.

Ignoring the key in my pocket, I went to town, lapping gently at her, bringing her to the edge and backing off more than once. Over and over I teased her until her arched back barely hit the mattress and she tangled her fingers in my hair to rub her pussy on my face in an effort to get herself off.

All the while I edged her until she cried out at the softest touch. Her clit pulsed against my lips as I kissed it gently, giving her nothing she needed and cleaning her messy thighs constantly with my tongue.

When she mewled at me, her heels catching under my shoulders and drawing me up, then I gave her what she needed, sucking her clit sharply into my mouth and biting gently.

She screamed–right into the palm I used to cover her mouth. Lori was tiny and in the bedroom we had fun with the size difference between us, learning to give each other pleasure and experimenting.

One of those things gave me the ability to stretch my much longer arm all the way to her mouth or throat as I pleased. I used my time cutting off her air while she came on my mouth, gushing a wave of hot cream I sucked and licked up, relentless while she screamed herself raw behind her hand.

Heady with her scent, I slid my way up her body, her nightdress hiked around her hips, one breast in my hand as I curled behind her fully clothed and kicked my boots off. She wriggled as I shucked my shirt, throwing it to the floor. The moment my skin touched hers, she sighed and settled.

*If that's what it takes.*

"Rest, baby. I'm not gonna stop, so rest now. Because I want to love you and punish you all at once."

She laughed at me–motherfucking laughed–and rubbed her round ass against my denim covered cock.

"Can't wait," she murmured sleepily, resting her cheek on my shoulder I tucked beneath her.

She fell asleep while I palmed her breast, kissed gently along her neck, and planned the best way to tease her next.

## CHAPTER FIVE

## LORI

I woke in the arms of a man I never expected to sleep with again. *Ever*.

No matter how many fantasies I actually harbored for Shannon, that day he walked out felt so... Final.

Yet here he was, freaking *spooning* me.

"I have to go to work." I wiggled a little, but his arms only tightened.

Flesh pressed to my back, muscle and tone I was familiar with, though as always he seemed larger than life.

"Liar," he whispered sexily in my ear. "I checked your calendar. You don't have anything."

There were a million ways to argue that one, but I had to say I admired his tenacity.

"You got into my calendar?" I frowned, though my heart pounded and I knew he felt the change in my body as he tucked me tighter to him.

"Does it matter? I'm here. You're here. So sleep well, for once." His breath brushed the slope of my shoulder, raising gooseflesh in its wake.

I wanted to argue that sleeping with him touching me like that was impossible, but when I closed my eyes and rested into the muscle of his shoulder, his hard heat pressed to my back, it was all too easy to push aside the fears, the arousal, and sink into him.

Just like I always used to do.

Coffee was the next thing to wake me, the scent of dark ambrosia with a dollop of cream right under my nose–literally.

"That smells divine." I reached back for Shannon, but he wasn't there.

Because he sat in front of me with a full hot breakfast on a tray–where the hell did he get a tray in my stunted kitchen? I never cooked.

"Morning, beautiful." He pushed the coffee into my hands and waved his fingers over the food. "Now, eat."

"That sounds like an order, and you know I don't do those so well first thing."

"Hence, the coffee."

I bit back an answering smile to his as those sky

blue eyes bore into mine, twinkling this time. "You're enjoying yourself way too much for this time of the morning."

"It's because of you." He leaned in, hesitating just a little in a way that made my heart swoop, and kissed my lips gently, pulling back before I could do something stupid.

*Like beg for more.*

Because the Shannon Incarsen I knew never hesitated. He was all in for everything he did. No questions, feet first, balls to the wall. That's why he was who he was.

The man I fell in love with.

I wasn't sure I recognised this version of Shannon before me, but my heart was far from complaining.

"This is a bad idea," I whispered over the lip of my coffee, and filled my mouth with the liquid before anything else fell out.

Shannon watched me drink my coffee with the eyes of a starving man, but he stayed back. "Eat," he repeated, softly.

I dipped my head and did just that, filling my stomach while my heart overloaded on the spot. About three bites in I stopped. "Aren't you eating?"

He shrugged. "I want you to eat first. Get the feeling you haven't been looking after yourself."

"Why do you get that feeling?" I looked down in case my bones were poking out and I missed it.

He was right, though. There were plenty of days I existed on snack bars between court appearances and worked well into the night. Today was a lull in an otherwise frantic work week. I'd planned to catch up with paperwork, and get some chores done but... spending it with Shannon, this version of him, suddenly didn't seem like such a bad idea after all.

"Because I know you, Lori. I know how hard you work. I know your expectations of yourself that exceed anyone else's."

My eyes narrowed. "I could say the same for you."

"But I want to look after you," he persisted. "I wanted to be here today, and make you smile."

My stomach swooped, leaving me high and dry.

Or wet and melting. Either way kinda worked for me because Shannon did what he always did, and left me in freefall.

He made a low noise in the back of his throat, slinking onto the bed to wrap his arms around me. "You gone cry on me, Lori? I ain't worth the tears, I promise."

"Too late," I sniffled, closing my eyes and fighting them back. "I gave too many tears to you when you weren't here."

A moment of silence filled my bedroom. Then–

"I was here. I saw them."

I closed my eyes and cried into my coffee for past me who thought he'd never hold me again, that my memories of him would always be distorted by magnificent sex and moments of loss with nothing between us but hard kisses.

"I shouldn't have walked out on you, Lori. I've never forgiven myself for that. Never." He kissed the tip of my shoulder.

"But you didn't come back. I- I waited," I confessed, back in a land where I was pathetic, and he was the hero.

And both of those versions were so, so wrong and not us.

He wasn't the hero. I managed just fine on my own. And I'd been wrong. It wasn't that I was lonely or tried to fill an unfillable space.

I simply missed *him*.

"I watched you move, remember? Three times." Shannon held his fingers in front of my face. "I didn't knock on your door because I couldn't handle your rejection, Lori. So much easier to give than receive, right?"

He nestled his chin on the top of my head, and we stared together out of the small window, its ledge cracked to let in a little air and probably how he got into my house in the first place, looking out at my small garden.

Small, but mine.

"I don't know if it can work again," I said desperately, clutching my trembling cup.

Warm hands engulfed mine, stopping my coffee from spilling over.

Shannon's legs formed a wide vee around my hips. "Do you want to try to make it work? I can't promise I'm not still a menace and I won't be sweet with you every time. But that frantic frenzy period? That's over. Training is most mornings, early. I haven't done galas since we split unless I'm up for a nomination. Games are a few months running for twenty-one weeks. And after that–"

"You're out for the night and the next day is recovery," I ended for him. "I remember how it works, Shannon. I lived with you for six years."

"No." A frown entered his voice, and I risked the existence of my coffee to twist in his arms to find him staring down at me, his gaze dark and intense.

That gaze got him on TV. A *lot*. The media loved the brooding, sulking asshole factor, and I married the alphahole within. Once, he even scared me, but now...

My body responded to him just as it did the day I walked back into the stadium and his first words were to ask if I was okay.

I nibbled my lip. *Maybe I'm doing this wrong.* I'd been so lost in what I needed that I forgot to ask what he needed, too.

Shannon's eyes hooded as he studied my mouth and a frisson of awareness rippled over my skin.

"What?" I whispered, pinned under his gaze.

"After every game I shower, I get my gear, and I come and find you. That's been my routine for three years. Since the day I walked out and felt like I couldn't come back." His arms tightened around me.

"You came to see me? Every time?" I sat, dumbfounded.

"After that first six months? Yeah." He scrubbed a hand behind his neck. "Watching you work became my balm." He shrugged behind me while I craned back at him, gawking. "My blood was high, exhaustion set in. So, I'd sit in my car and watch you and eat, or I'd come right up to the window like a kid at a toy store, looking at something locked away behind glass he could never have."

My tears changed, my heart breaking for him. "Oh, God. Shannon. You should have knocked. I–"

"Would you have let me in?" He uttered a harsh laugh that raised hairs along the back of my neck. "The man who turned his back on you instead of listening like I fucking well should have?"

"If you had knocked–" I didn't get anything else out, as per usual.

"You would have slapped my face, and probably called the cops. Be real, Lori," he said irritably, locking eyes with me.

I took a deep breath. "I would have let you in."

"Bullshit."

That stung.

"No, you listen to me, you overgrown man-child with more muscles than any girl has a right to ever touch," I burst out, glaring back at him. "Three years you're saying you could have given me my greatest wish–you, on my doorstep, maybe an apology on your lips, wanting to come in and talk after your game? Or, more, maybe," I faltered as he leaned closer, catching the back of my neck in his fist and pulling me right onto him.

The food trays and my coffee hit the carpet in a clatter, and I didn't look back to see the mess.

"Talk? You think talk was what I wanted from you?" His eyes bored into mine.

"So it's sex, always sex?" I taunted, knowing I was pushing him in all the right/wrong ways. He was a beast of a man, and I was a girl scout with a stick.

A really short, flimsy stick.

"Yeah." He pulled me closer, flattening our bodies together. "I wanted to fuck you. Broke into your fucking house so many times I've lost count to kneel by your bed, kiss you and touch you and got the fuck out before you saw my face. Those were the new memories I made, fucking my fist to the sounds of you coming in your sleep." His breath came ragged, his chest heaving against my chest. "You're saying instead of haunting your building like a fucking memory, I could have come inside and had all that with you?"

I swallowed hard. "Yes."

"Fuck." He stared at me for a long moment, unmoving.

Then his mouth crashed down over mine, his tongue invading, fists tearing. My nightgown lay in shreds, his hands everywhere on my bare skin. Shannon didn't waste a moment in kissing me to worry about things like where we were. His cock pressed hard to my entrance and before I could protest I wasn't ready, he surged forward, filling my very much not dry pussy with his thick cock, impaling my heart in the process.

He set about railing us both into a future I couldn't see yet but sure as hell wanted with the man who sat beneath my window, crept to my bed to steal kisses and offer pleasure I could barely grasp in the mornings, but never, not once, hurt me.

"I fucking love you so goddam much it hurts, you know that?" he rasped over me, pushing me onto my back and bearing his weight over me.

"I love you," I admitted, trying not to gasp as he thrust deeper, again and again. "I thought it– oh God, Shannon, I thought it had to be perfect but I was wrong. So wrong," I cried out.

"We'll make the time you need. I promise. But you're mine, and you stay mine, you understand?" A flicker of insanity entered his gaze as I nodded. "Words, Lori. Be a good girl and use them for me."

"I'm yours," I promised back, my voice trembling as I added a caveat of my own. "But you're mine, too. It goes both ways."

He smiled at me, a full, Shannon Incarsen smile that told me he had exactly what he wanted and was proud of me for getting there with him. I swore I melted on the spot, or maybe I sizzled. He groaned, slamming his body against mine until our moans mingled and he shouted my name to the world while I curled in the safety of his embrace, the loneliness chased away by the man who haunted my bed, and came back to stay.

# CHAPTER SIX

## SHANNON

Having Lori in my arms beat every feeling I experienced since the day I walked out on her in the biggest mistake of my life. And damn if I refused to fuck up with her again. She forgave me for stalking her, for breaking into her house, for watching her. All the things she shouldn't but the craving that brought us together was a two-way ravenous street.

I spent the day holding her, loving her a hell of a lot gentler than when I lost my shit earlier, and I got to watch her curl up beside me and fall asleep while I fixed a few emails that couldn't wait, and let Coach know I needed a little more time for family.

He said okay.

I wasn't the first on the team to have a long-term fixture and I think he knew I wasn't done with her. Hell, most of them had that opinion, but the only one blind enough not to see it was me.

"You wanna move to the bedroom, baby?" I looked down at her, but Lori was well gone, completely out.

Her body softened against mine as I shifted the borrowed laptop to the other end of the sofa and slid my arms easily beneath her.

She weighed less than a feather, I swore, and she'd always been tiny, but by God did tiny pack a punch. Lori took everything I gave and came back for more–literally. This morning she creamed on my cock at least three times before I couldn't hold back, marking her inside as mine again, this time with her permission.

And fuck me did that feel good.

It would be a challenge to see how her life in the little cottage that tried to mirror ours from a lifetime ago would fit with my uptown apartment, but we'd manage. Hell, I'd live here with her, if she let me. But now was the time for taking big changes slow, our renewed truce so fragile I didn't want to shatter what we created with an accidental breath.

But she let me back in and she fucking loved me. Hearing those words tumble from her lips might have been the best moment of my life to date.

I hefted her gently just as her tinny doorbell rang and cut out. I frowned, adding that to a growing list of repairs she either didn't have the energy to do or didn't care. I wanted her home to be the perfect haven for her. Maybe we could keep both and buy something else for the two of us. It wasn't like I had anything else, or anyone, to spend my stupidly high income on from the team and promotions I agreed to do.

"Be right there," I called softly, placing her back on the sofa, laying her head on a pillow.

The doorbell rang again, and I cursed as I stumbled over a few discarded pillows from where we made love on the floor earlier.

"Coming, motherfucker," I muttered, hoping her mailman or whoever it was understood when something wasn't urgent.

But when I opened the door, a pale, round face atop a brown suit beamed up at me.

"Dateless Dave."

"Mister Incarsen." He bobbed on his toes, his smile growing ever larger. "I did want to meet you. I'm here for my date with Lori, of course." He nodded to himself and managed to duck under my arm and into her house.

I rubbed the back of my neck, unsure how to remove the man, unwilling to wake her or get handsy with anyone. If Lori wanted a quiet life together, that meant staying out of the media. I was good with that, but this–this was a potential clusterfuck in the making.

"Uh, I don't know what your arrangement was, but we're back together. So, no more dates and she's asleep in there," I pointed at the living area, "So, it's time to go, Dave."

He spun on his heel to face me, his plump, reddening face still beaming. "Oh, I know she's not expecting me. Just like she wasn't expecting you for all those times, too."

I blanked. "What?"

He shrugged genially and put a bag on the ground reaching for something while he talked and my brain tried to play catch up. "I didn't know if you'd want to do her together, or how your tastes ran. But I am a big, big fan, Mister Incarsen. Your biggest."

I blinked at the little dude. "Right. That's great. Uh, door's there. I think we should let her sleep and all while she can."

"Of course, of course. But I'm not leaving." Dave edged toward the doorway that led to her, around me.

Bile rose in my throat. "You don't go in there." My hands fisted at my sides while I tried to calculate the likelihood of breaking the man's neck if I picked him up sideways and tossed him out of her front door.

Then I decided I didn't care anyway and stepped forward.

Dave sighed. "I was afraid this might happen. I'll change my plans, but only because it's you." He brought a canister out from behind his back and squeezed.

The spray hit me dead in the face. "The fuck is that," I growled, waiting for my eyes to water, or my chest to close up.

Nothing happened. Except the little guy smiling like a fucking creeper at me. His words rippled around my head as the room wavered.

*Just like she wasn't expecting you for all those times, too.*

Jesus. I encouraged this guy who was already watching her, clearly well before their date. This was *my fault.* The room swirled around me, and my knee hit the deck, but I didn't feel anything.

"The fu-"

That's all I got out before Dave appeared in my field of vision, pressing a fingertip to my forehead.

And I fell backward.

## CHAPTER SEVEN

### LORI

I woke up with no warmth around me, and my hands and feet were cold. Really cold. So was the rest of me.

I stared at the open window, the night sky above, the thin curtains billowing in the breeze and shivered. "Shut that," I mumbled, or tried to, but something large was in the way.

I chewed down and the thing gave, but didn't budge. My tongue explored whatever Shannon shoved in my mouth–this time–and came to the conclusion it was a ball gag.

*I remember what nights like this were like.*

But he never left me freezing cold before. Maybe he wanted to play around with temperatures, but my feedback was that this was *not* the best way to do it.

At least I hadn't woken up in a damn ice bucket. Shannon was partial to those things, swore it helped with recovery and all, but I couldn't make myself get into it. Comfort all the way for this girl.

Fingers trailed up my thighs, already damp with my ruminations, and traced over my pussy lips. I swallowed, and only managed to add a fresh strand of drool to a small pool at the back of my throat that trickled slowly towards my breasts. My nipples peaked as the investigative fingers slowly entered me, my cold hands and wrists spread wide on the bed, in cuffs that rattled when I tried to shift and free myself.

Another moan built as I turned my head toward Shannon, and came up with a face that should never have been in my house. I froze, my joints locking up, my pussy clenching with the wave of fear that flushed me hot and cold all over.

"You're tight and so reactive," Dave gushed, working his fingers inside my wet pussy.

Wet, because I thought it was another man who touched me.

But it wasn't Shannon touching me now.

I tipped my head side to side, screaming through the ball but I only managed to mangle the sound into a series of gurgles that probably made it no further than the open window.

"So truly beautiful. All for me," Dave murmured, his face aglow with rapture as he played with my nipples and worked his fingers in and out of my pussy.

I choked on my spit—or it might have been

vomit—jerking my body away but he came too, crawling his clothed body on top of mine.

"You're as soft as I remember. Isn't that right, Mister Incarsen?" Dave called gently, like waking a lover.

My head thrashed to the other side, finding Shannon tied to one of my dining table chairs, his arms bound behind himself with rope and duct tape, including over his mouth.

*Please don't let it hold him.*

I prayed the short prayer with all my might as he shook his head experimentally once, then twice. I screamed again, the pathetic sound ripping my throat as Dave rubbed his crotch on my belly.

Bile built, but Shannon's eyes flickered open, focusing on the man writhing on top of me and he *roared.*

Through the tape. The sound reverberated around the room, and Dave moaned in response.

"I didn't think having you here would be as fun, but if you want to share her, I'm good with it. Paint her with our cum, smear it in her blood when I carve her up for you?" he offered like I was some roasted meat proffered to a special guest.

*"ET OFF ERRRRR!"* Shannon yelled, ripping at

the ropes that bound him. The chair creaked, but nothing gave any sign of giving way.

Dave sighed. "I did hope it would be better. Now I'll just have to do it alone." His stilled fingers worked inside me again. "Should I incite the beast within, make you come for me?"

I shook my head, every limb trembling as I realized my body was cold because I lay on plastic that covered my bed.

*Plastic to catch the mess as he kills me.*

The revelation left me screaming and crying, and whimpering when the frenzy departed me. But his touch didn't stay light and clammy and unwanted as he brought one of my clit sucking toys out of his bag and toward my skin, flicking it on.

I heard the vibrations before I felt them, and tears tracked down my face as I shook my head frantically.

"OOO. Onuchhheee," I cried, everything garbled between my fear, my locked body and the gag distending my jaw, pushing my tongue back.

"Oh yes. He showed me, you see. Long before I approached you I was following Mister Incarsen, and he brought me to you. Slipping into your room, running his hands over your body, making you moan in your sleep. Coming on you." He rubbed his clothed body over me, moaning.

I shook violently, my head turned away, seeking Shannon.

His eyes bulged, his face red as he tore at the bonds that held him back. The chair creaked beneath him and I nodded frantically. Shannon paused, cocking his head to one side and rocked experimentally. Something else creaked and he twisted harder, throwing himself over on one side.

Dave groaned on top of me and something wet hit my thigh.

I cried out like it hurt, but disgust crawled up my throat. I swallowed back vomit, unwilling to drown in it and do the job for Dave by accident.

Maybe I should have because a second after he got himself off, his fingers still jammed inside me, he pressed the clit vibe home. Right on cue the little piece of magical tech did its job in a horrendously efficient way.

My orgasm hit me hard, ripping through me and mingling all my fear at being an unwilling participant in this horrific nightmare flooding me. I gushed all over the plastic sheet, sobbing through the wave of pleasure as Dave panted down at me. The vibe rolled to one side as something flashed in my vision.

The cold knife tip pressed between my breasts, drawing down over my belly.

I screamed behind my gag as the blade bit into my skin, trailing all the way to my pussy. Dave smiled, his face wavering through my tears as he positioned the blade between thighs and pressed it up into my entrance.

"Now I'll see how you really scream," he promised, his face full of holy glorification, like I was the sacrifice at an altar of his choosing to a god who never recognised him.

I opened my mouth wide, yanking at the cuffs frantically, prepared to do exactly that as a shadow slammed across the top of my bed and suddenly Dave was gone.

My head thrashed to the other side. Shannon launched himself, still half taped and roped, over Dave, the blade in his hand. It raised and my throat dried.

"OOOooo!"

Shannon didn't look at me. "He's gotta go, Lori. He touched you."

"Iioouuttteeeeeddddia," I said logically.

Shannon huffed at me, busting one piece of matchstick that used to be part of one of my dining chairs away to free his other arm, pinning Dave down with a knee to his chest.

I almost felt sorry for Dave. Shannon's thighs were legendary material. Then he threw a punch that Shannon blocked, and I didn't feel bad for him any more at all.

Shannon pulled his phone out of his pocket and dialled. "Police please," he said politely, holding the knife away, Dave tucked under his knee, part of a chair still taped to his ass.

And he was the sexiest damn sight I'd ever seen.

# EPILOGUE

## SHANNON

*Six months later.*

It took weeks for the media storm to die down that kicked in the moment the cops walked through Lori's door and decided to snap a selfie. Unprofessional, but I got it. What scared the shit out of me was losing an already traumatised girl because of my fuck ups.

But it took more than a weird date, a knife and an unwanted visitor abusing her to take my Lori down. She fell into my arms the moment I freed her from those fucking cuffs–and threw them at the cops as evidence. They weren't coming back, and I was good with it. We could be kinky in our own damn way without them.

The moment she was in my arms Lori checked me over, ignoring the poor female cop trying to get her rape kit together. I batted her hands away and wrapped her in my arms, whispering apologies while I cried shamelessly for the woman who suffered on my behalf.

She didn't give a fuck, pushing the cops and media back out the door the moment they were all done, and locked it behind herself before launching at me.

We took it gentle these last months, merging our lives in a hurry and selling the cottage she used to love...right up until I did the thing that I never expected to be able to give her–the first house we bought listed for sale, and I bought it. Her name was on the deed, though she didn't know it, and now I got to drive her to our destination. Her eyes were covered with a black silk tie of mine–best I could do on short notice–and I parked right in front of the house. I took the sale sign away earlier, and the lawn was freshly mown.

"Are we here?' she asked breathlessly, her hand wrapped around mine.

I nodded, swallowing down the lump in my throat. "Let me get the door."

She waited patiently while I got the door, helped her out and brought her to the middle of the yard.

"Feels squishy."

"Yeah." It was the only word that came out.

"Are you okay?' she frowned, turning blindly up at me, and it was time.

"I'm good," I lied as I kissed her cheek and loosened the tie around her eyes.

Her blindfold fell off and she gasped, gripping my hand tight, frozen to the spot. "Is this-" She leaned back and checked the dented mailbox I made myself when I hit a puck at it and got the damn thing once. "Oh, my God. It is. Did you..?" she trailed off, unsure, a question in her eyes.

I grinned like a madman, pulling her in close to me. "Yeah, I bought it. For us."

"You bought it back. A second time."

"For everything," I finished for her, finding her lips in a gentle kiss. "Always."

"Always," she repeated more strongly. "Got a key?"

"Yeah. Something else first." I paused, my hand in my pocket, wrapped around the key. *Now or never, Incarsen.* "First, I wanna ask you something."

"What?" She peered up at me, practically bursting at the seams to get back into the house we owned a long time ago.

"First, I want to ask you to marry me...again," I said softly, producing the art deco diamond band that matched her wedding ring and slid it on her finger. "Will you marry a poor hockey player?"

"Poor in timing, maybe," she snorted. Her smile faltered. "You mean it?"

I nodded. "That first wedding was all family, friends and all the things you do in your twenties. I want this one to be somewhere quiet, and just us."

She nibbled her bottom lip, looking up at me through her lashes and arousal surged through me. "Just us? You mean it?"

It's what she always wanted, and I'd give her every inch of the earth and the moon and the stars if it made her happy.

"Yeah. I mean it."

Lori nodded, running her finger across the band. "Okay?"

"You'll do it? Marry me again?"

"I mean, I know we don't have to, but it'd be fun, and a new start, and–"

I cut her off with a hard kiss that left her trembling, until I realised the trembles were giggles.

"Way to put a man in his place, Lori," I muttered, flicking her nose.

She ducked under my arm and dashed into the house, the key from my pocket glinting in her hand.

I shook my head and followed, letting her have a head start. She'd need that for when I caught up with her and did all the dirty things a man could do with his wife while he told her he loved her with his mouth, hands and tongue.

And we could always go a second round.

Yeah, she'd like that.

Thank you for reading Shannon and Lori's second chance romance. Please do leave a review. Even one line of your thoughts helps. It really does.

Jericho Chimeras' Captain Hux is up next
with a snowed in bratty Valentine's romance
Read PUCK MY HEART

If you'd like more super steamy and dark hockey
romance
the boys of the Rippton Allstars are waiting.

Power Play Off the Ice...where the action melts the ice, on and off the rink!

This May and June, things heat up on and off the ice!

Join seven of your favorite romance authors and get in on the action...

Puck Me Twice by Allie Lasky

Shut Up and Puck Me by Wynter Ryan

Puck me Already by Kat Obie

Puck Me Always by Sofia Aves

Puck Me Harder by Ariana St. Claire

Puck Me for the Win by Annee Jones

Power Plays don't always happen on the ice. And sometimes, everyone wins in love.

Follow us on Instagram at Power Play Off the Ice!!

# ABOUT THE AUTHOR

USA Today Bestselling author Sofia Aves writes fast-paced police romances, sizzling military units, steamy cowboys with a Montana backdrop and the occasional cheeky god. Married to a veteran, she often tackles topics of PTSD and reintegration and has a soft spot for all who work in uniform. Sofia writes kidlit for charity and has over one hundred and fifty publications across four not-so-super-secret pen names.

Publishing is her life. As acquisitions editor for Evernight and Evernight Teen Sofia loves discovering new and established author voices in romance. She is a mum of three crazies in a returned veteran household and has a pair of overly large fur babies who think they're teacup puppies.

Sofia lives near Brisbane, Australia and has her own alpaca park, Lorendel.

www.sofiaaves.com

Sign up to Sofia's newsletter and get a free Blue Blooded Brothers book.

Haven't read the Z Boy's prequel? Get it for free here:

A TABLE FOR TEN

www.sofiaves.com

Follow Sofia on

Amazon

BookBub

Instagram

Goodreads

Tiktok

**Read Sofia's Series**

Blue Blooded Brothers

Red Hart Ranch

Texan Devils

Z Boys

Klauss Brothers

Sundae Dreaming

Australian Customs Security

Writing spicy paranormal romance as

RAVEN HUSH

Club Fray

**Monster Brides**